TIDES AND TERRITORIES

SEA AND WILD ANIMALS

MOONSTONE

Published in Moonstone
by Rupa Publications India Pvt. Ltd 2024
7/16, Ansari Road, Daryaganj
New Delhi 110002

Sales centres:
Bengaluru Chennai
Hyderabad Jaipur Kathmandu
Kolkata Mumbai Prayagraj

P-ISBN: 978-93-90260-51-5
E-ISBN: 978-93-90260-52-2

First impression 2024

10 9 8 7 6 5 4 3 2 1

Printed in India

CONTENTS

SEA ANIMALS

CONTENTS

WILD ANIMALS

SEA AND WILD ANIMALS

SEA ANIMALS

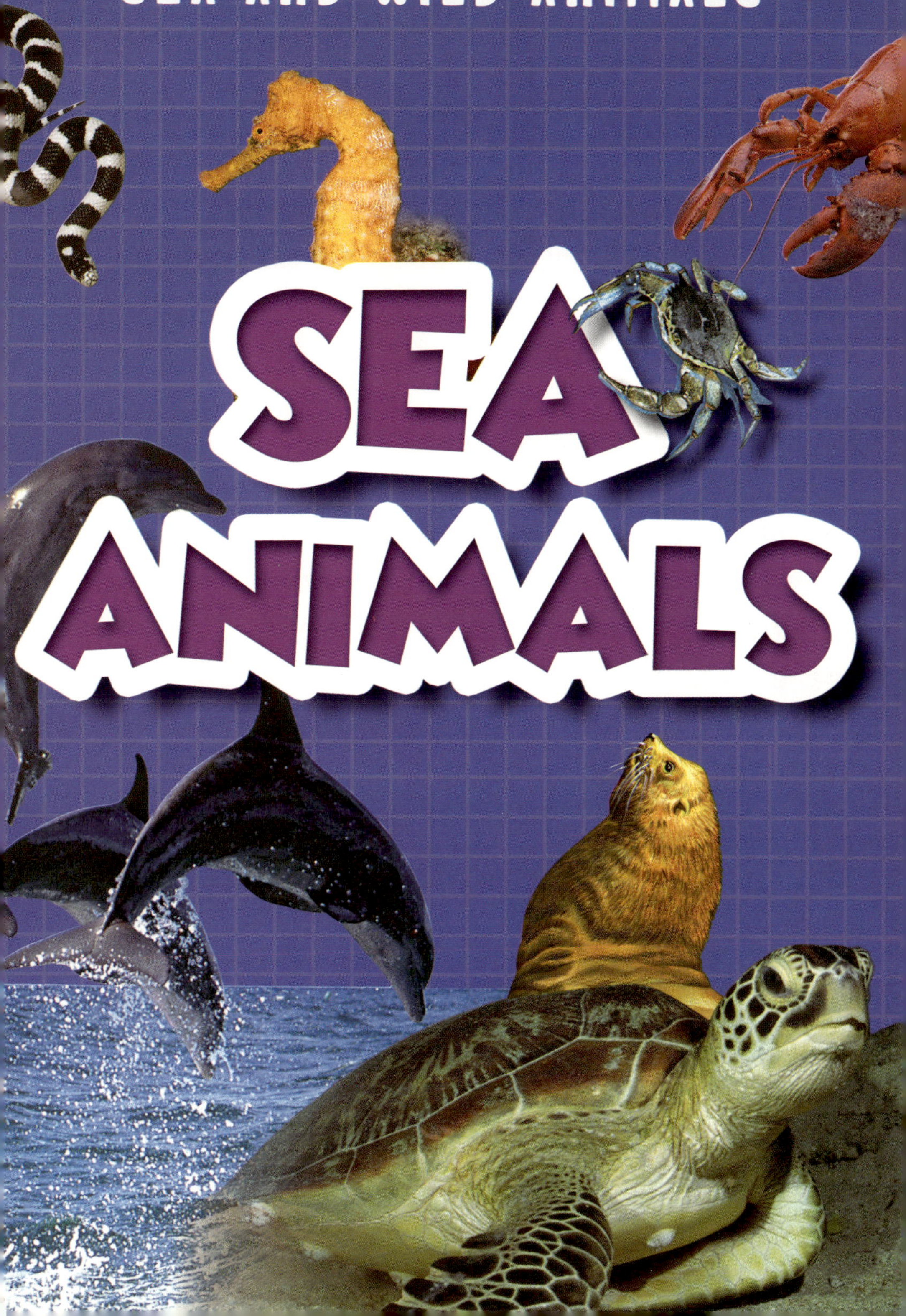

Introduction

Seas and oceans together cover approximately 71 percent of our planet. Many amazing creatures inhabit these seas and oceans. The number of sea animal species discovered so far is approximately 242,500 and millions more are yet to be found.

Sea animals range from microscopic zooplanktonnes to the world's largest animal—the blue whale. Life appeared in the seas millions of years ago. Jellyfish and sponges were two of the first sea creatures. Today, multiple species of fish, invertebrates and mammals live in seas and oceans.

Coral

Corals are marine animals that live in colonies. There are two types of coral: hard coral and soft coral. Hard corals are the primary reef-building corals, and soft corals do not form reefs. Coral reefs can spread for thousands of miles under the sea.

Coral Species

Corals appeared around 570 million years ago. There are of 6,000 species of corals in the seas today. About 2,500 of them are hard coral animals.

Coral Polyp

A coral polyp has a sac-like or cylindrical-shaped body. It has a single opening, or mouth, surrounded by stinging tentacles called cnidae or nematocysts. When a prey passes by, the tentacles use these cells to stun and kill the prey.

Coral Reefs

Coral reefs are vibrant and diverse underwater ecosystems, gardens of coral polyps found in tropical seas. Many animals, such as sponges, blacktip reef sharks, clown fish, eels, parrotfish and clams (such as giant clams) take shelter in these coral reefs. In addition to providing these animals with a home, the coral reefs also provide them with food.

Facts

- Coral reefs are known as the rainforests of the sea.
- In the Great Barrier Reef, there are more than 4,000 species of mollusks, 1,500 species of fish and 400 species of corals.
- Coral reefs provide food and livelihood to more than 500 million people.

Great Barrier Reef

The largest coral reef in the world is the Great Barrier Reef, which is located off the coast of Australia. It consists of more than 3,000 reefs and covers an area of more than 300,000 square kilometres (about 115,831 square miles).

? ________ reef is the largest coral reef in the world.

Coral Reef Animals

Coral reefs provide food and shelter to myriad species of animals. They cover about one percent of the ocean floor but support about 25 percent of marine life. Animals vary in their interactions with the reefs; some are transient visitors, while others are permanent residents.

Coral Reef Fish

Reef fish are well-adapted to life among coral reefs. Their bodies are often flattened to navigate the complex coral structures, and they display a wide range of vibrant colours, which is in contrast to the typically silvery colours of open-water fish. Common reef fish include clownfish, angelfish, butterflyfish, surgeonfish, and damselfish.

Sponges

Sponges, which are multi-cellular organisms, play an essential role in coral reef ecosystems. They are of various colours and shapes. They filter water and process nutrients, thereby maintaining the health of the reefs. The pores in the outer walls of sponges help in drawing water and filtering out food and oxygen. As water flows out, it carries out waste and carbon dioxide.

Facts

- Sponges do not have muscles, a nervous system, or a circulatory system.
- Clownfish are also called anemone fish.
- Sea snakes also inhabit the coral reefs.

Other Reef Animals

Coral reefs host various animals, including sea worms like flatworms, Christmas tree worms, feather duster worms, crustaceans like shrimps and crabs, cephalopods like octopuses, and larger predators like reef sharks. Sea urchins, jellyfish, oysters, sea anemones, dugongs, and sea turtles also thrive in coral reef environments.

? Coral reefs provide _______ and shelter to various reef animals.

Shrimps and Prawns

Shrimps and prawns are crustaceans. Crustaceans are animals with ten legs and hard exoskeletons. Both of them are bottom dwellers and are found in both freshwater and marine water.

Shrimps

There are more than 2,000 species of shrimps on earth. Shrimps are sandy in colour and bury themselves in sand. They grow up to the length of a few millimetres to nine inches (20 cm). They have a light-weight exoskeleton and muscular abdomen which helps them swim. Shrimps swim backwards by quickly bending their abdomens and tails.

Shrimp Farming

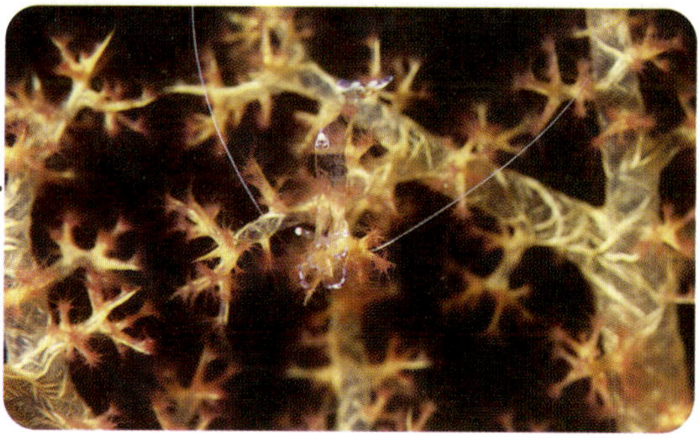

The farming of aquatic animals is called aquaculture. Shrimp farming is one of the most popular businesses in the world. Shrimps and prawns are favourite sea food items and are farmed in large quantities for human consumption. Thailand is the world's leading exporter of shrimps in the world.

Prawn

Prawns closely resemble shrimp but are a little larger than them. They have branching forms of gills, which makes them different from shrimps. Prawns grow up to 13 inches (33 cm) and can weigh up to one pound (450 grams). They have toothed beaks, long antennas and their eyes points forward from the head.

Facts

- Snapping shrimp or pistol shrimp is one of the loudest animals on earth.
- Shrimps and prawns are favourite sea food items around the world.
- A shrimp's heart is found in its head.

? **Are prawns a little larger than shrimps? Yes or No**

Crab

Crabs are animals with flattened bodies and a hard shell. They have four pairs of legs and a pair of claws for catching food and fighting enemies.

Hermit Crabs

Hermit crabs live in the empty shells of snails to protect themselves. They move to bigger shells when they grow. A hermit crab's abdomen goes into the shell while its legs and claws remain outside.

Blue Crab

Blue crabs are the most commonly grown creatures. They have a brown-coloured shell and sapphire-tinted claws. A female blue crab has red tips on its claws.

Good Swimmers

Some crabs have paddles on their last pair of legs, which makes these crabs good swimmers. Other crabs can walk and run sideways over sand or rocks.

Facts

- Horseshoe crabs can swim upside down in the open ocean.
- The pea crab is the smallest crab, with a measurement of 0.25 centimetres (about 0.09 inches) across the shell.
- Kelp crabs have slim legs and powerful claws, which help them to move around.

? Name the smallest sea crab in the world.

Lobster

Lobsters are creatures related to crabs. They have long, slender bodies, eight walking legs, and a pair of large claws.

Bottom-dwelling

Lobsters mostly spend their lives at the bottom of the sea. Some lobsters live in the rocky crevices, while others hide among the sea grasses.

Atlantic Lobster

Atlantic lobsters are large, heavy lobsters. They weigh more than 9 kilograms (about 20 pounds). Once, an Atlantic lobster even weighed over 19 kilograms (about 42 pounds)!

Hunting Lobsters

Lobsters walk along the ocean bottom as they hunt for food at night. They eat animals such as worms, clams, mussels, crabs, and fish. Some lobsters even eat other lobsters.

California Spiny Lobster

California spiny lobsters do not have claws for protection like other lobsters. Instead, they have spines on their shells to protect themselves from predators.

Facts

- Lobsters can swim backwards by flipping their tails to escape from their enemies.
- Most lobsters reach a length of 30 to 60 centimetres (about 1 to 2 feet).
- American and European lobsters are the most commonly eaten lobsters.

? California spiny lobsters have spines for protection. True or False

Dolphin

Dolphins are large mammals like whales. They have streamlined bodies like fish, but they are not fish. They breathe air and give birth to young ones like other mammals.

Echolocation

Dolphins communicate with the help of echolocation. They send sound waves, which reflect back after striking their prey. Dolphins then catch the reflection and detect the prey around them.

Dolphin Colour

Dolphins are generally gray-coloured. They have darker backs and lighter underbellies.

Smallest and Largest

Currently, Hector's dolphin is the smallest dolphin species. It is only 11.2–1.6 m (3 ft 11 in – 5 ft 3 in) in length and weighs about 40–60 kg (88–132 lb). The largest dolphin species is the orca or killer whale. It can grow to a length of more than 9 metres (about 30 feet).

Playful Creatures

Dolphins are known for their playful nature and intelligence, often leaping out of water. Sometimes, they follow ships and match their movements with one another.

Facts

- There are more than one million common dolphin species worldwide.
- A dolphin can eat more than 13 kilograms (about 30 pounds) of fish in a day.
- Dolphins can jump to a height of 6 metres (about 20 feet) out of the water.

What is the largest dolphin on earth?

Jellyfish and Man-of-War

Jellyfish are simple animals. They have a soft, transparent, bell-shaped body. Tentacles grow out from the edges of their body.

Stinging Cells

Jellyfish have stinging cells on their tentacles, which provide them with protection and help them gather food. When the tentacles come into contact with a prey, the stinging cells inject the poison into it.

Australian Box Jellyfish

The Australian box jellyfish is the most poisonous jellyfish. It has 15 tentacles growing from each corner. Each tentacle reaches a length of three metres (about 10 feet) and has 5,000 stinging cells. A box jellyfish stings its prey and pulls it towards the mouth inside its body.

Portuguese Man-Of-War

The Portuguese man-of-war is not a jellyfish. It is actually a siphonophore, a colony of organisms with a gas-filled float. The float is purple-blue in colour. Long tentacles hang out from the float. The tentacles are about 9 to 18 metres (about 30 to 60 feet) long. Portuguese man-of-war use there poisonous tentacles to kill prey such as fish and other small animals and draw them to the float.

No Tentacles

Some jellyfish, such as the cannonball jellyfish and the mushroom jellyfish, do not have tentacles. Cannonball jellyfish have round, white bells bordered with a brown or purple colour.

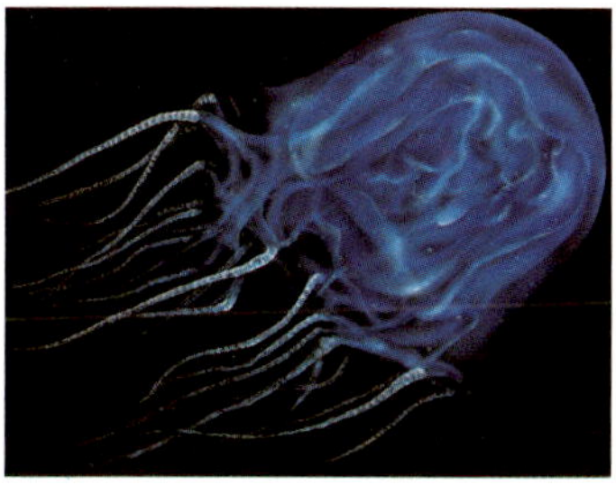

Facts

- A large box jellyfish's venom is enough to kill about 60 people.
- A jellyfish's body is made of 98% water.
- There are about 2,000 species of jellyfish throughout the world.

? **Portuguese man of war is a jellyfish. Yes or No**

Octopus and Squid

Octopuses and squids are mollusks. Octopuses have eight long arms and squids have ten long arms. They have suckers on the arms to grip objects and their prey.

Defensive Actions

Octopuses can match the colour, pattern and texture of their bodies to their surroundings. They have special muscle and pigment cells on their skin that change colour. This defensive action helps them avoid predators, such as sharks, eels, and dolphins. Sometimes when they get caught, they blow out a cloud of black ink on the enemy to escape.

Movement of Squids

Squids draw water into their bodies and force it out through their backs with the help of a funnel near the neck. This helps them to move their bodies through the water.

Giant Squid

The giant squid is one of the biggest invertebrates on earth. The largest giant squid ever found was 13 metres (about 43 feet) in length and weighed over 900 kilograms (about 1,980 pounds).

Blue-Ringed Octopus

The blue-ringed octopus is highly venomous enough to kill a human being in a few minutes. It is pale brown to yellow in colour, but shows blue rings all over its body when alarmed.

Facts

- Giant squids have the largest eyes in the animal kingdom.
- Octopuses can squeeze their soft bodies into small cracks and crevices.

How many arms does an octopus have?

Eel

Eels are snake-like fish. They have elongated, thin bodies, like snakes. They have smooth skin with scales and thin fins along the body.

Home of Eels

Eels usually live on coral reefs and in sandy or rocky areas. They are found in tropical and temperate waters across the world.

Young Eels

Female eels lay eggs in the sea, which hatch into transparent larvae known as leptocephali. The larvae swim to the shallow waters and grow into tiny eels called elvers. Elvers travel to the freshwater in groups and spend most of their lives there. They migrate back to the sea to reproduce.

Garden Eel

Groups of garden eels look like seagrass. They remain buried in the sand with their heads up while hunting. They catch fish and other small animals as they pass by. These garden eels immediately move back under the seabed when a predator approaches.

Moray Eel

Moray eels lead a solitary life and live in small holes in the coral reefs. There are many species of moray eels. All moray eels have sharp, razor-like teeth varying in shape and size to eat their prey and kill their predators.

Facts

- Eels produce a slimy substance when threatened. It helps them slip away from their predators.
- Female eels die after laying eggs.

? Name the eels that look like sea grass.

Sea Snakes

With streamlined bodies and paddle-like tails, sea snakes are well adapted to living in the oceans and seas. They are usually found in the warm waters of the Indian Ocean and Pacific Ocean.

Characteristics of Sea Snake

Sea snakes do not have gills and hence have to come up to the surface to breathe. After taking a gasp of air, they can stay underwater for 20 to 30 minutes. Their paddle-like tail helps them swim swiftly. Some sea snakes can dive 100 metres or more and can remain underwater for up to 80 minutes.

Eating Habits

Sea snakes use their venom to kill their prey and swallow them whole. Their skull bones are loosely attached and they are capable of dislocating their lower jaw and moving it sideways to swallow larger prey. They usually dine on fish, fish eggs, crabs, prawns and other animals.

Facts

- Sea snakes are sometimes mistaken for eels because of their similar appearance.
- Like land snakes, sea snakes also shed their skin after every two to six weeks.
- Sea snakes have valves in their nostrils which they close while diving underwater.

Banded Sea Snake

Banded sea snakes are very poisonous as their venom is ten times more toxic than that of a rattlesnake. However, these sea snakes are meek creatures and do not usually bite humans if they come across them. They usually live in the mangrove swamps and shallow tropical waters of coral reefs. Unlike other sea snakes, banded sea snakes are amphibious and can spend ten days on land. They usually come to shore to mate and lay eggs.

? Sea snakes breathe through gills. True or False

Shark

Sharks are large, carnivorous fish. Their skeletonnes are made of cartilage. Cartilage is a tough elastic tissue. Most sharks have slate-grey skin and a slender body. Over 500 species of sharks are found worldwide, comprising one percent of all the fish.

Whale Shark

The whale shark is the largest fish. It grows to a length of 5.5 to 10 metres (about 18 to 32 feet), but even this huge size does not make it a threat to humans. Whale sharks feed on plankton and tiny creatures by filtering them from the water.

Shark Food

Most sharks are predators and feed on other fish. Large sharks, like the great white shark, feed on mammals, such as seals and dolphins, large fish, turtles and seabirds. Sharks mostly hunt at night.

Hammerhead Shark

Hammerhead sharks get their name from their hammer-shaped heads. They have their eyes and nostrils on each of the ends of the head. Great hammerhead sharks are the largest hammerhead sharks and one of the largest sharks in the world.

Facts

- Blue sharks are known to migrate the longest distance, 3,058 to 4,345 kilometres (about 1,900 to 2,700 miles).
- There are over 500 species of sharks that are known to scientists.
- Spined pygmy sharks are one of the smallest sharks, with a maximum known length of 20 to 25 centimetres (7.8 to 9.8 inches).

A shark's skeleton is made up of ________.

Ray

Rays are fish related to sharks. They have flat, thin bodies with long tails. Their fins extend from the sides of their heads to the end of their bodies. Rays slowly flap their fins to move forward.

Ray Colour

Rays are grey-brown in colour, which helps them camouflage on the ocean bottom. Deep water ray species are usually dark-coloured while shallow water species are light-coloured with wavy lines (which look like waves).

Stingray

Stingrays have a long spine on their backs to protect themselves from predators. The stinging spine extends from the back halfway along the tail. Stingrays also produce venom from their underside, which is deadly enough to kill human beings.

Manta Ray

The Giant Manta Ray is the largest ray in the world with a wingspan of upto 26 feet. The width of the disc of a manta ray is greater than its length. Manta rays are good swimmers and they are also sometimes seen leaping out of the water and gliding.

Food Habit of Manta Rays

Manta rays are filter feeders. Like filter feeding sharks, they swim about with their mouths wide open and gulp in gallons of water along with plankton and tiny fish.

Facts

- Eagle rays use their poisonous bony spines to pierce their predators.
- Baby rays are ready to take care of themselves immediately after birth.
- Rays do not sleep, but only switch between rest and activity.

? What is the largest ray in the world?

Seal and Walrus

Seals and walruses are large mammals. These animals are known as pinnipeds, which include seals, sea lions and walruses. Walruses have two long white tusks. Seals and sea lions do not have tusks.

Walrus Tusk

Walruses have tusks that are about 1 metre (about 3 feet) long. The tusks can be even longer in some males. Male walruses use their tusks for fighting. Both male and female walruses use their tusks as hooks for climbing on ice and for digging out their food, such as shellfish.

Largest and Smallest

The Southern Elephant Seal is the largest seal, weighing more than 4,000 kilograms (about 8,800 pounds). The smallest seal is the Biakal Seal, which weighs 50-130 kilograms (about 110-290 pounds).

Differences

Sea lions have external ears, unlike seals and walruses. All pinnipeds have fin-like feet or flippers for movement. Seals have rear flippers that point backward and help them move in a vertical motion. Sea lions and walruses rotate their hind feet forward under the body and move by supporting their body on the limbs.

Stellar Sea Lion

Stellar sea lions are the largest sea lions. Sea lion pups are born with a dark brown coat, which becomes reddish-brown as they develop. Stellar sea lions feed on octopuses, squids, fish, and on other seals and seal pups.

Facts

- Between the two species, Pacific and Atlantic walruses, the former is the larger one.
- The Hawaiian monk seal can dive more than 50 times in a day and can hold its breath for 20 minutes.
- Male elephant seals are two times larger than female seals.

? **Seals, walruses and sea lions are ________.**

Sea Cow

Sea cows are mammals that live in tropical waters. They have large, thick bodies with flippers and a tail. The flippers help them swim in water and move food towards the mouth. Dugongs and manatees are sea cows. Dugongs have a fluked tail while manatees have a round, paddle-shaped tail.

Sea Cow Food

Some sea cows eat algae and floating plants while others often eat shellfish and dead fish. Adult sea cows can eat about 13.6 kilograms (about 30 pounds) of food in a day.

Sea Cow Size

Dugongs grow up to 3 metres (about 10 feet) in length and weigh about 400 kilograms (about 880 pounds). Manatees may grow up to be more than 4 metres (13 feet) in length and weigh 400 to 500 kilograms (880 to 1,100 pounds). The largest manatee was found in Florida. It was 4.6 metres (about 15 feet) in length and weigh 1,600 to 1,700 kilograms (3.520–3,740 pounds).

Manatee

Manatees are slow-moving, gentle animals. They are often seen body-surfing or barrel-rolling while playing. They communicate with each other by squealing underwater to show fear or excitement. Manatees generally spend most of their time eating and relaxing.

Dugong

Adult dugong males have two small tusks, which they use in fighting with each other. They also have sensitive bristles on their large snout. They use them to find sea grass.

Facts

- Baby dugongs must swim to the surface of water to take their first breath.
- Manatees are solitary animals, but may form groups of 12 or more.
- Dugongs have poor eyesight, but they have an acute sense of hearing.

? **Is manatee a sea cow? Yes or No**

Seahorse

Seahorses are fish. However, they do not look like fish. They have a horse-like snout and an upright body covered with bony armor. Seahorses can be 1.5 to 35 centimetres (about 0.6 to 13 inches) long.

Male Mothers

Male seahorses give birth to young ones instead of females. They have a brood pouch on their belly where the females lay eggs. The male carries the eggs until they hatch.

Snout and Tail

Seahorses have a unique snout and tail. As plankton and small-shelled animals pass by, they get sucked in by the seahorses. The prehensile tails of seahorses attach them to the corals and sea grasses.

Seahorse Fin

Seahorses have a small fin on their back. It helps them propel themselves in water. This fin flutters about 35 times in a second. Small fins on the back of their heads also help them push through the water.

Pygmy Seahorse

Pygmy seahorses are only 1.5 centimetres (0.6 inches) in length. They have a short snout and bulb-like tubercles on their body. Pygmy seahorses belong to the coral reefs of the western Pacific, including Australia. They are camouflaged in the corals by their purple or yellow colour.

Facts

- Seahorses can consume 3,000 or more brine shrimp per day.
- The potbelly seahorse is one of the largest seahorses, growing up to more than 30 centimetres (13.7 inches) in length.
- At one time, 200 young seahorses hatch from the male seahorse's body.

? ____________ sea horse gives birth to young ones.

Sea Turtle

Sea turtles are aquatic reptiles. They have soft bodies covered with a shell and have large flippers. Sea turtles cannot pull their legs and heads inside their shells like tortoises.

Seven Species

There are seven species of sea turtles—green, hawksbill, olive ridley, Kemp's ridley, flatback, loggerhead and leatherback. The Kemp's ridley is the smallest sea turtle, weighing only 36 to 45 kilograms (79 to 99 pounds). Leatherback sea turtle is the largest sea turtle. It is 1.8 metres (about 6 feet) in length and weighs more than 900 kilograms (about 1,980 pounds).

Loggerhead Turtle

Loggerhead turtles are known for their large heads and powerful jaws. The power of their jaws helps them crush the mollusks and crabs inhabiting the coral reefs and rocks.

Life Cycle

Although sea turtles spend most of their lives in the water, females come ashore to lay eggs in the sand. After laying the eggs, they cover them and return to the sea. The incubation period for the eggs is about two months. The hatchlings emerge at night and make their way to the sea, where they spend the rest of their lives.

Facts

- Olive ridley turtles are named for the olive colour of their shell.
- Adult green sea turtles are the only sea turtles that eat plants.

? Name the largest sea turtle in the world.

Sea Star and Sea Urchin

Sea stars are star-shaped invertebrates with multiple arms projecting from a central disc. Sea urchins are round, hard animals covered with spines.

Tube Feet

Tube feet are small tube-like projections on starfish and sea urchins. They help them propel themselves along the sea floor.

Crown-of-thorns

Crown-of-thorns starfish are venomous starfish with long and sharp spines. The spines grow up to a length of 4 to 5 centimetres (1.5 to 2 inches). They are usually multicoloured, ranging from purple with red-tipped spines to green with yellow-tipped spines.

Starfish Species

Around 2,000 species of starfish or sea stars live in all the oceans of the world. All sea stars have at least five arms. Some may have as many as 30 arms.

Lost Arms

Sea stars can regenerate their lost limbs. If they lose an arm, some sea stars are capable of regrowing it, and in some cases, a lost arm can regenerate into a new sea star.

Facts

- Starfish can push their stomachs out of their mouths to swallow bigger prey.
- Sea urchins use their spines as defensive weapons and for catching prey.
- The sunflower star is one of the biggest starfish, with 40 centimetres long (over 15.7 inches) arms.

? ________ **star fish has about two inches long projections.**

Whale

Whales are large mammals found in all oceans of the world. They are the biggest creatures on earth. They have long bodies with smooth skin.

Flippers and Flukes

Whales have paddle-shaped flippers. Most whales have dorsal fins on their backs and tail fins known as flukes. The flukes propel them through water.

Great Migrators

Gray whales migrate great distances in groups known as pods. They travel about 20,000 kilometres (about 12,427 miles) from the cold waters of Alaska to warm waters.

Beluga Whales

Beluga whales can be easily recognized by their unusual white colour. They are also known as white whales. The calves are born gray and change their colour to white as they mature. Belugas are popular for their sounds, such as whistles, clangs and clicks. They can also mimic other sounds.

Blue Whale

The blue whale is the largest animal that has ever lived on earth. It grows to a length of 30 metres (about 98 feet) and weighs more accurately, over 200,000 kilograms (about 200 tonnes). This enormous animal feeds on tiny animals known as krill. Blue whales have about 400 baleen plates with bristles, which trap krill when these whales swim with their mouths open. A blue whale can eat about 4 to 8 tonnes of krill in a day.

Facts

- Whales breathe through nostrils known as blowholes that are on the top of their head.
- Blubber is the layer of fat under the skin in whales.
- The lyrical sounds made by most whale species are loud and can be heard from many miles away.

What is the largest animal on earth?

Glossary

Abdomen: the part of the body that contains the stomach and reproductive organs

Bristles: short and stiff thick hair

Clam: a hard-shelled animal that lives in shallow water

Colony: a group of plants or animals living together

Crevice: a crack in the rock surface

Enemy: an organism that poses a threat or is antagonistic to another

Invertebrate: an animal without a backbone

Mammal: an animal that gives birth to babies and feeds them with milk

Mimic: to copy or imitate

Mollusk: invertebrates with soft bodies, often with shells, including snails, clams, and octopuses

Pigment: a substance that gives colour to something

Plankton: very tiny plants and animals found floating in the seas and oceans

Predator: an animal who kills and eats other animals for food

Prehensile Tail: a tail that can wrap around objects and hold onto them

Prey: an animal who is eaten by predators

Rainforest: a forest in an area where it rains a lot

Reflection: throwing back of sound, light or heat from a surface

Regenerate: to re-grow a lost part

Shellfish: a shelled animal, such as a clam or a lobster

Solitary: preferring to be alone

Sucker: a round structure on the body of the octopus that helps it to stick to surfaces

Temperate: neither very cold nor very hot

Tropical: very hot and humid regions located near the tropics

Tubercle: small, round projections on an animal's body

Venom: poison produced by animals

Answers

Page No. 9	Great barrier
Page No. 11	Food
Page No. 13	Yes
Page No. 15	Pea crab
Page No. 17	True
Page No. 19	Killer whale or orca
Page No. 21	No
Page No. 23	Eight
Page No. 25	Garden eels
Page No. 27	False
Page No. 29	Cartilage
Page No. 31	Manta ray
Page No. 33	Pinnipeds
Page No. 35	Yes
Page No. 37	Male
Page No. 39	Leatherback sea turtle
Page No. 41	Crown of thorn
Page No. 43	Blue whale

SEA AND WILD ANIMALS

WILD ANIMALS

Introduction

Wild animals include all non-domesticated animals, such as wild cats, dogs and elephants. These animals live independently in the wild. Some wild animals live in social groups while others prefer to live alone.

Wild animals are found in almost all kinds of habitat—from the arid sun burnt deserts to the snow-capped mountains. They may be carnivores—meat eating, herbivores—plant eating or omnivores—both plant- and meat-eating.

Lion

Lions are large powerful predators found in parts of Africa and Asia. They are one of the largest wild cats. They have nothing to be afraid of, except human beings. Hence, they are often called the "king of the jungle."

Lion's Mane

Adult male lions have long, shaggy manes around their necks. Male lions start growing manes around the age of two, and they are typically fully formed by around 4.5 years. The lion is the only cat to have a mane.

Pride

Lions are the only cats that live in groups. A group of lions is called a pride. A pride may have up to 20 members, which include around a dozen lionesses and their cubs and one or two lions. The males protect the cubs and the territory, while the females do most of the hunting.

Hunting and Diet

Lions often hunt together in groups. Female lions are the main hunters in a pride, and they prey on large animals like wildebeests, zebras, and antelopes. After a hunt, all members of a pride share the food. When food is scarce, lions are also known to steal food from hyenas and wild dogs.

Facts

- A lion spends almost 21 hours in a day sleeping and resting.
- Lions can survive without water for 4 to 5 days.
- The American lion, or Panthera atrox, lived from around 340,000 to 11,000 years ago and went extinct approximately 10,000 years ago.

What is a group of lions called?

Tiger

Tigers are the largest members of the cat family and have a distinct striped coat and a white belly. Tigers are the only cats to have striped fur. Tigers live in the tropical evergreen forests, woodlands and grasslands of Asia (from India to the eastern parts of Russia).

Amur Tiger

The Amur (Siberian) tiger is found in the Boreal forests of China, North Korea and Russia, is the largest tiger. Amur tigers are an endangered species. There are less than 4,000 of them living in the wild.

Endangered Animals

Tigers are endangered animals. In the early 20th century, there were nearly 100,000 tigers living in the wild. Today, it is estimated that around 4,500 survive. Hunting and loss of habitat have reduced their population in most areas. Tigers are killed for their beautiful coat and body parts.

Bengal Tiger

The Bengal (Indian) tiger is the most common subspecies of tiger. It is found in Bangladesh, Bhutan, China, India, Myanmar and Nepal. India has the highest population of Bengal tigers.

White Tiger

White tigers are born when both parents have unusual genes for white colouration. They are not found in the wild. They are bred in captivity in wildlife parks and zoos around the world.

Facts

- The stripes on a tiger's body are like the fingerprints of humans; no two tigers have the same pattern of stripes.
- A tiger's roar can be heard from as far as three kilometres (about 2 miles) away.
- The Sumatran tiger, found in Sumatra, Indonesia, is the smallest sub-species of tiger.

? Which is the smallest tiger?

Cheetah

Cheetahs are the fastest animals on land. Their slender bodies and long legs are well-suited for the great speeds at which they chase their prey. Cheetahs live in the grasslands of Africa and parts of Iran.

Spots and Tear Stripes

The beautiful, spotted coat distinguishes cheetahs from most other large wild cats. Cheetahs also have black "tear marks" that run down the sides of their nose to their mouth.

Facts

- Cheetahs can sprint up to 114 kilometres per hour (about 71 miles per hour).
- Cheetahs do not roar like lions, but they purr, hiss, whine, growl and make bird-like chirping sounds.

Food Habits

Cheetahs hunt early in the morning or late in the evening when it is not too hot. They are carnivorous, preying mainly on small to medium-sized antelopes, hares, birds, and rodents.

Cubs

Female cheetahs can give birth to up to nine cubs at a time. When born, cheetah cubs are blind and have a thick silvery-grey mantle on their backs, which they eventually shed. The cubs stay with their mother until they are about 13–20 months old.

What marks do cheetahs have on their face?

Bear

Bears are large, powerful mammals found in parts of Asia, America and Europe. They have large bodies, stocky legs, long snouts, small, rounded ears, shaggy hair, paws with five nonretractile claws, and short tails.

Lifestyle

Bears like to spend most of their time alone, hunting for food and eating. Most bears are fast runners, excellent swimmers, and good climbers. Bears living in the cold regions hibernate during the winter season.

Great Grizzly

The grizzly bear, or the great Alaskan brown bear, is the largest bear. It lives in the cool mountain forests and river valleys of Alaska and Canada.

Smallest Bear

Found in the tropical and subtropical forests of Asia, the sun bear is the smallest bear. Sun bears are great climbers. They even make their homes up in the branches of trees.

Polar Bear

Polar bears are large, white bears that live in the islands and coasts of the Arctic Sea. They are the largest meat-eating land animals. Polar bears are perfectly suited to their lives in the cold Arctic. Their bodies are covered with thick fur, and they have a thick layer of fat beneath their skin that protects them from the cold.

Food Habits

Bears eat plants, grass, roots, berries, large insects, and fish. Some large bears hunt mammals, such as moose, caribou, and elks, too. Polar bears live entirely on fish and seals, while the sloth bear, which is found in India and Sri Lanka, feeds entirely on termites.

Facts

- Grizzly bears may weigh up to 680 kilograms (about 1,496 pounds).
- The American black bear is the most common species of bears.
- Asiatic black bears are often trained to dance and ride bicycles for human entertainment.

? **Which is the largest meat-eating animal?**

Giant Panda

The giant panda is a black and white bear with a round head, heavy shoulders, a stocky body and a short tail. Giant pandas are found in the mountains of western, and southwestern China.

Behaviour

Giant pandas are solitary animals. They rarely interact with each other. They socialise only during the breeding season.

Diet

Pandas are carnivores, but they have switched to a vegetarian diet. They feed exclusively on bamboos. Pandas spend 10 to 12 hours a day eating bamboo and consume between 12 to 38 kilograms (about 26 to 84 pounds) of bamboo in 24 hours.

Endangered

The giant panda is one of the most endangered animals on earth. Habitat loss and hunting has reduced its population. There are only about 1000 to 2000 giant pandas surviving in the wild today.

Conservation programs

China has taken many steps to protect the vulnerable giant panda. The panda is considered a national treasure in China and is provided with the highest category of legal protection. China also has about 40 panda reserves where these beautiful bears have a safe shelter.

Where do you find giant pandas?

Facts

- China has more than 50 panda reserves that have been built to protect the animal.
- The giant panda is the symbol of World Wildlife Foundation (WWF).

Canids

Canids belong to the Canidae family, which includes dogs, wolves, foxes, coyotes, and jackals. All canids are carnivores.

Arctic Fox

The Arctic fox is a canid that lives in the Arctic region. Arctic foxes have a white-coloured coat in winter, which they shed for a brown one in summer. They live in burrows or dig into the snow to shelter themselves.

Coyote

Coyotes are wild dogs found in North America. They have a long, grey-brown to yellow-brown coat and thick white fur on their bellies.

Facts

- Coyotes are very good swimmers.
- Dingoes, considered wild dogs, are native to Australia.
- Jackals are medium-sized wild dogs found in Africa, Asia, and southeastern Europe.

Gray Wolf

The gray wolf is the largest wild dog. Gray wolves are found in different kinds of habitat, ranging from the deciduous forests of North America to the frozen Arctic of Siberia.

African Wild Dog

African wild dogs are medium-sized wild dogs with large, round ears and a coat marked in shades of brown, black, and beige. They live and hunt in groups called packs.

? Which is the largest wild dog?

Hippopotamus

Hippopotamuses, large animals with short, stumpy legs, are among the largest land mammals, following elephants and rhinoceroses. They are found in parts of Africa.

Two Species

There are two species of hippopotamus—the river hippopotamus and the pygmy hippopotamus. The pygmy hippopotamus is smaller than the river hippopotamus.

Lifestyle

The river hippopotamus can be found near rivers and water bodies in grasslands. They spend much of their time in the water or wallowing in mud. They often remain submerged in water with just their eyes, ears, and nose above it.

Food Habits

Hippopotamuses are herbivores. They feed on grass, vegetables, and fruits.

Sticky Skin

The skin of a hippopotamus secretes a pink-coloured liquid that protects its skin and prevents it from cracking when it is out of water and in the sun.

Facts

- A hippopotamus can weigh up to 4,500 kilograms (about 9,900 pounds).
- Hippopotamuses have been around for the last five million years.
- Female hippopotamuses are smaller than males.

? **Hippopotamus are the __________ largest land animals.**

Rhinoceros

The rhinoceros is a large, horned animal with stumpy legs. It lives in the grasslands of Africa and Asia. There are five species of rhinoceros—Sumatran, Javan, Indian, Black and White. The Sumatran, Javan and Indian rhinoceros are found in Asia while the Black and the White rhinoceros are found in Africa.

Indian Rhinoceros

The Indian rhinoceros is found in the grasslands and forests of Nepal and Assam, India. It can be distinguished from the African rhinoceros by its single horn and its skin, which falls into deep folds at the joints.

Lifestyle

Rhinoceros spend most of their time during the day wallowing in lakes, rivers, and muddy water. This keeps their body cool. They are usually active at night or in the early morning when it is not very hot.

White Rhinoceros

The white rhinoceros (square-lipped rhinoceros) is the most common species of rhinoceros. It is the second-largest land animal after the elephant.

African Rhinoceros

The African rhinoceros has two horns and is larger than the Asian rhinoceros. Both the black and the white African rhinoceros are usually the same colour—gray.

Facts

- All rhinoceroses are herbivores.
- The male white rhinoceros can weigh up to 3,500 kilograms (about 7,700 pounds).
- The Javan rhinoceros is the rarest species of rhinoceros.
- Rhinos are hunted for their horns, which many people believe have medicinal qualities.

Which is the most common species of rhinoceros?

Elephant

Elephants are the largest land animals. They are found in the grasslands and forests of Asia and Africa. There are three living species of elephants— the African forest elephant, the African bush elephant, and the Asian elephant. The African elephant is the largest land animal.

Tusk

An elephant's tusks are the two long, upper teeth that are located towards the front of its mouth. They are made of ivory. Elephants use their tusks to dig up roots; tear the bark of trees; and to protect themselves.

Trunk

The trunk of an elephant is its long, flexible snout. The trunk has two nostrils at its end, which help it breathe. Elephants use the trunk to eat food and drink water. They also use it to spray water over their bodies and to trumpet.

Asian and African

African elephants can be distinguished from Asian elephants by the overall size and shape of their ears and tusks. The ears of African elephants are large and shaped like the African continent; while the ears of the Asian elephants are shaped like the Indian subcontinent. The tusks of African elephants are longer, and their skin is darker than that of Asian elephants.

Facts

- A single tooth of an elephant can weigh more than five kilograms (about 11 pounds).
- Human beings kill elephants for their ivory tusks, which are very valuable.
- An adult elephant can eat up to 136 kilograms (about 299 pounds) of food in a day.

? How much food can an adult elephant eat in a day?

Zebra

Zebras are black and white striped animals found in the grasslands of Africa. They belong to the horse family. There are three living species of zebras—the plains zebra, the Grévy's zebra, and the mountain zebra.

Plains Zebra

The plains zebra (common zebra or Burchell's zebra) is the most common species of zebra. It is found in eastern, southwestern, and southern Africa. Plains zebras live in social groups that consist of a stallion and a few mares and foals. The stallion oversees the group.

Unique Stripes

The stripes on all zebras are unique. No two zebras have a similar coat. The stripes of a zebra help it to camouflage itself and make it difficult for predators to pick out one single animal from a running herd.

Quagga

The quagga is an extinct species of zebra. It had brown and off-white stripes on its head and neck. It also had a white belly and legs. Quaggas were hunted to extinction for their meat and hide. The last quaggas died in the 1870s.

Facts

- A zebra can rotate its ears without moving its body.
- The Grévy's zebra is the largest species of zebra.

? **Which is the most common species of zebra?**

Deer

Found almost everywhere on earth except in Antarctica and Australia, a deer is a flexible-bodied, cud-chewing mammal. Deer are fast runners and excellent swimmers. Most species of deer have antlers.

Antlers

Antlers are horn-like, external organs that grow on the head of a deer. In all species except the reindeer, only male deer have antlers. The reindeer is an exception as female reindeer also have antlers.

Indian Muntjac

The Indian muntjac is one of the most common species of deer. It is found in India, Sri Lanka, Nepal, Myanmar, Thailand, Vietnam, Malaysia, and the Indonesian islands of Java, southwestern Sumatra, and Borneo.

Musk

Musk is a substance with a strong odour secreted by the musk deer. It is used in medicines and perfumes.

Largest and Smallest

Deer are small to medium-sized mammals. Some deer, such as the European elk or the moose, are more than two metres (about 7 feet) tall while the South American pudu grows up to a height of just 25 centimetres (about 10 inches).

Facts

- There are about 50-60 species of deer.
- A male deer is called a buck, stag, or bull; a female deer is called a doe or cow; an a young deer is called a fawn or calf.
- Deer hunting is a popular sport in many countries.

? Which is the most common species of deer?

Antelope

Antelopes are even toe-hoofed animals. They are among the fastest animals on earth. Antelopes roam the grasslands, woodlands, and marshlands of Africa. They are herbivores and feed on grass, leaves, and seeds. They live in herds of 20 or more animals.

Eland

Elands are the largest antelopes. They are usually reddish brown in colour and have spiraled straight horns. A female eland's horns are longer and thinner than the male eland. Male elands have tuft growing from their dewlap (loose skin that hangs down from the neck).

Thomson's Gazelle

Thomson's gazelles are beautiful antelopes with ringed horns. They are light brown in colour with black markings on the sides, white underbelly and rump. Male Thomson's gazelles are larger than females and set up their own territories. They protect their territories by fighting off their rivals.

Royal Antelope

Royal antelopes are the smallest antelopes. They are about the size of a rabbit. They are light brown in colour with paler underbellies and dark-coloured heads. These small antelopes are shy, nocturnal animals. They are solitary animals and spend most of their time alone.

Facts

- Many antelopes hide their babies in tall grasses or rocks to protect them from predators.
- Only male royal antelopes have small spike-like horns.
- The leaping of antelopes by lifting all four legs is called stotting or pronking.

? Which is the largest antelope on the Earth?

Giraffe

Giraffes are the world's tallest land animals. They have long legs, which are 1.8 metres long (about 6 feet), a sloping back, and a very long neck. Giraffes inhabit the open grasslands and woodlands of Africa.

Spotted Coat

Giraffes possess a striking sand-coloured coat with dark brown patches. The patches can be large or small. No two giraffes have the same pattern on their skin. The pattern also differs from species to species. The coat helps them camouflage themselves. While grazing in the open, they often look like dry trees from a distance. This protects them from predators.

Facts

- Giraffes can run at almost 48 kilometres per hour (about 30 miles per hour).
- Giraffes have hair-covered horns known as ossicones on their heads.

Acacia Leaves

Giraffes spend most of their time browsing the leaves of tall trees, like acacia and myrrh. Their long necks enable them to browse these trees easily. The leaves satisfy their hunger and also provide them with enough moisture to quench their thirst.

Males are Taller

Male giraffes are taller than female giraffes. They grow up to five to six metres (about 16 to 20 feet) tall, while most females are 4.8 metres (about 16 feet) tall.

? Where do giraffes live?

Marsupial

Marsupials are a group of animals in which females have a pouch called a marsupium. Marsupials carry their babies in the pouch. Marsupial babies are born before they are fully developed. After birth, the baby climbs into the pouch, where it feeds on the mother's milk and grows.

Koala

Koalas (koala bears) are tree-dwelling marsupials found in Australia. They live in eucalyptus trees in the eucalyptus forests of Australia. They only feed on eucalyptus leaves.

Opossum

Opossums are medium-sized marsupials found in North America. Opossum babies are almost the size of honeybees when they are born. After birth, they climb into their mother's pouch, where they remain until they are about 70 to 125 days old.

Kangaroo

Kangaroos are large marsupials that live in the grasslands and forests of Australia and its neighbouring islands. There are more than 60 different kinds of kangaroo. The red kangaroo is the largest of them all.

Which are the largest marsupials?

Facts

- The red kangaroo can hop up to 48-64 kilometres per hour (about 30 to 40 miles per hour).
- A male kangaroo is called a boomer and a baby kangaroo is called a joey.
- Wallabies are small or medium-sized kangaroos found in Australia.

Gorilla

Gorillas are the largest apes. They are shy and peace-loving animals found in the jungles of Africa. After chimpanzees, gorillas are the closest living relatives of human beings.

Food Habits

Gorillas are primarily vegetarians. They eat leaves, stems, fruits, seeds, and roots. Sometimes they also eat worms, ants, termites, and other small insects. Gorillas spend most of their time eating. In fact, it is their favourite pastime.

Facts

- Gorillas sleep for about 13 hours every night.
- Gorillas are one of the most endangered animals.

Troop

Gorillas are social animals. They live together in groups of up to 30 gorillas. A group of gorillas is called a troop. The troop is led by a strong male called the silverback. Silverbacks are named for the patch of silvery grey hair on their backs.

Babies

Newborn gorillas depend on their mother for food and care. Gorilla babies can usually walk within three to six months after birth.

? What is a group of gorillas called?

Chimpanzee

Chimpanzees are apes. They live in the rainforests, grasslands, and woodlands of Africa. They grow up to four feet in height and weigh about 90 to 120 pounds (41 to 54 kilograms). They feed on fruits, seeds, buds, insects, and eggs.

Social animals

Chimps are friendly and lively animals. They live in large groups that consist of up to 60 members. They make different types of sounds and are one of the most noisy animals. They also smile, laugh or cry and make gestures for communicating with other chimps.

Use of Tools

Chimpanzees are smart animals. They use twigs to take out termites and insects from trees. They use stones as hammers to smash open hard nuts. They even use leaves as sponges to soak drinking water.

Baby Chimps

Baby chimpanzees stay with their mothers for as long as ten years. The mothers may feed them and play together to keep their young ones safe.

Facts

- Chimpanzees belong to a group of animals called primates.
- Almost all chimpanzees make nests in the trees for sleeping at night.
- Like humans, chimpanzees can stand upright and walk for shorter distances.

? Chimps live in ________.

Crocodiles and Alligators

Crocodiles and alligators belong to the same group of reptiles called crocodilians. Both of them are good swimmers and look almost alike. However, they can be distinguished by the shape and structure of their snouts. Crocodiles have long and narrow snouts whereas alligators have wide and broad snouts.

Structure

Crocodiles and alligators are cold-blooded animals which mean that they regulate their body temperatures according to their surroundings. To warm themselves they bask in the sun and to cool themselves they bask with their mouths open or stay in water.

Facts

- Crocodiles have a unique hole called foramen of panizza in their heart which helps them to control their breath underwater. This hole allows them to shut their heart and slow it down to one or two beats per minute.
- Alligators and crocodiles use their tail to propel themselves through water.

American and Chinese

Alligators usually live in freshwater habitats but sometimes they are also found in brackish water. There are two types of alligators – American alligator and Chinese alligator. American alligators are larger than Chinese alligators. On an average, American alligators grow up to 10 to 15 feet (three to five metres) where as Chinese alligators are about five feet long.

Saltwater Crocodile

Saltwater crocodiles are one of the largest reptiles on land. On an average, saltwater crocodiles grow up to 17 feet (five metres) and weigh about 1,000 pounds (450 kilograms). They live in the brackish and saltwater areas of eastern India, Southeast Asia and northern Australia. These crocodiles dine on almost any animal that comes their way, including monkeys, buffalo, wild boars, etc.

? What is the largest reptile on land?

Extinct Wild Animals

Extinction is a natural process. It occurs when a population of species dies out faster than they are born. Extinction can be triggered by natural events as well as by various human activities, such as poaching and the clearing of forests.

Mass Extinctions

Our earth is around 4.5 billion years old. During this period, there have been around five instances when almost all species of plants and animals were wiped out. The first mass extinction occurred 438 million years ago, and the last mass extinction occurred 65 million years ago when large animals, such as dinosaurs, disappeared.

Dinosaurs

Dinosaurs were large reptiles that roamed the earth during the Mesozoic Era. They died out 65 million years ago due to natural causes.

Miss Waldron's Red Colobus

Miss Waldron's Red Colobus was a red and black-coloured monkey that was found in West Africa. The monkey has not been seen by anyone since 1978 and was declared extinct in 2000. According to the International Union for Conservation of Nature (IUCN) redlist, the colobus monkey is listed as critically endangered under criteria A2cd; C2a(i); D.

Mammoth

Mammoths were huge elephant-like animals that lived during the Ice Age. They became extinct around 11,000 years ago. Mammoths were more than three metres (about 10 feet) tall and had long, curved tusks. They had a hairy coat and a thick layer of fat under their skin that kept them warm.

Facts

- Since the 1600s, about 500 species of animals have become extinct.
- The Andrewsarchus, or Andrews' beast, was the largest carnivorous land mammal that lived in parts of Asia around 32-60 million years ago.

? **How many years ago did mammoths become extinct?**

Glossary

Brackish Water: water that is salty but not as salty as sea water

Browse: to graze on or nibble at the leaves of trees

Camouflage: to have physical features that blend an animal into its surrounding environment

Deciduous Forests: forests in which trees shed their leaves in a particular season

Endangered: an animal that is on the verge of becoming extinct

Extinct: something that no longer exists

Grassland: a wide area of land with grass and small plants

Hibernate: to sleep during the winter months

Ice age: a period when the earth was covered with ice

Mane: long, rough hair around an animal's neck

Marshland: a land partially submerged in water

Mesozoic Era: a time period in which dinosaurs dominated the land

Nimble: very swift and agile

Pastime: any activity that is done during spare time

Poach: to illegally kill animals for commercial purposes without government permission

Pouch: a small bag-like cavity

Propel: to push something forward

Secrete: to release or produce

Solitary: living alone

Sprint: to run very fast, usually for a short distance

Stumpy: short and thick

Subcontinent: large part of a continent

Termite: a very small insect that eats wood, often referred to as white ant

Wallow: to roll about in mud or in water

Woodland: a wide area of land with trees

Answers

Page No. 51	Pride
Page No. 53	Sumatran Tiger
Page No. 55	Tear marks or tear stripes
Page No. 57	The polar bear (on land)
Page No. 59	Mountain ranges of central China
Page No. 61	Grey wolf
Page No. 63	Third
Page No. 65	White Rhinoceros
Page No. 67	136 kilograms (299 pounds)
Page No. 69	Plains Zebra
Page No. 71	White-tailed deer (North America)
Page No. 73	Eland
Page No. 75	Savannas and woodlands of Africa
Page No. 77	Kangaroos
Page No. 79	Troop
Page No. 81	Africa
Page No. 83	Saltwater crocodile
Page No. 85	11,000 years ago